Oh Where, Oh Where Has My Little Dog Gone?

D1223732

SMITHSONIAN INSTITUTION

To my loving husband, Gregg, and our two adventurous dogs.—E.P.V.

Book copyright © 2008 Trudy Corporation and the Smithsonian Institution, Washington, DC 20560.

Published by Soundprints, an imprint of Trudy Corporation, Norwalk, Connecticut.

All rights reserved. No part of this book may be reproduced or transmitted in any form or by any means whatsoever without prior written permission of the publisher.

Editor: Laura Gates Galvin
Book design: Meredith Campbell Britton
Production coordinator: Chris Dobias
Audio design: Brian E. Giblin

First Edition 2008
10 9 8 7 6 5 4 3 2 1
Printed in China

Acknowledgments:
  Soundprints would like to thank Ellen Nanney at the Smithsonian Institution's Office of Product Development and Licensing for her help in the creation of this book.

Library of Congress Cataloging-in-Publication Data

Villnave, Erica Pelton
  Oh where, oh where has my little dog gone? / illustrated by Erica Pelton Villnave ;
  edited by Laura Gates Galvin.—1st ed.
          p. cm. — (American favorites)
  Summary: An illustrated presentation of the well-known song about a missing dog.
  Includes historical notes, classic and new lyrics, and a short biography of the
  nineteenth-century songwriter, Septimus Winner.
  ISBN 978-1-59249-859-8 (hide-n-seek book) — ISBN 978-1-59249-860-4 (pbk. book)
  1. Children's songs, English—United States—Texts. [1. Songs. 2. Dogs—Songs and music.]
  I. Galvin, Laura Gates, 1963- II. Title.

PZ8.3.V725Oh 2008
782.42—dc22
[E]

                    2008017115

Oh Where, Oh Where Has My Little Dog Gone?

Edited by Laura Gates Galvin
Illustrated by Erica Pelton Villnave

Soundprints®
Where Children Discover...

Oh where,
oh where
can he be?

With his ears cut short

and his tail cut
long,

oh where,
oh where
can he be?

I love my doggie, oh so much,

and my doggie,
I know he loves me.

He's my **very** best friend

and I miss him so...

My doggie has come back to me!

Oh Where, Oh Where Has My Little Dog Gone?

Traditional

Oh where, oh where has my lit - tle dog

gone? Oh where, oh where can he be?

With his ears cut short and his tail cut

long, oh where, oh where can he be?

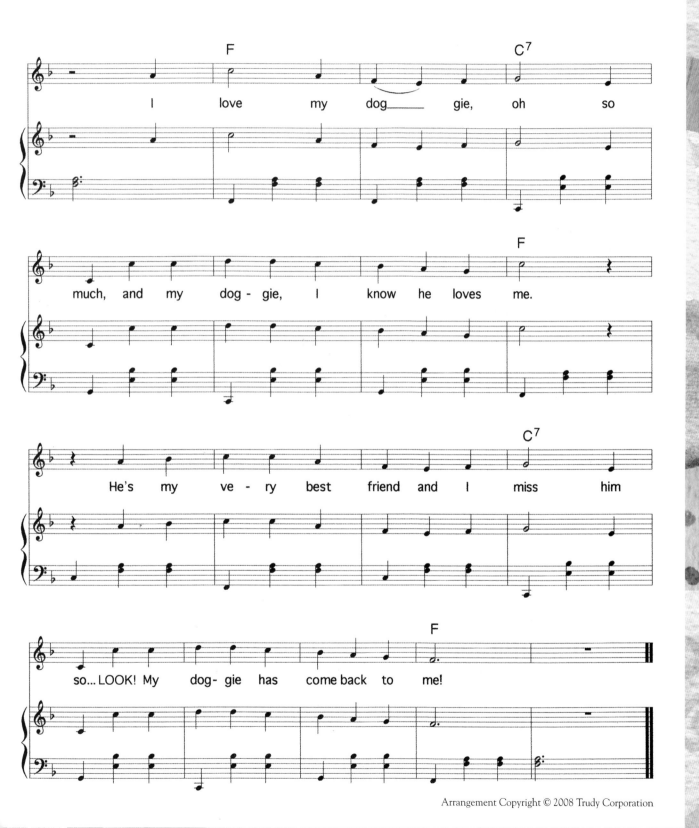

I love my dog___ gie, oh so much, and my dog - gie, I know he loves me.

He's my ve - ry best friend and I miss him so... LOOK! My dog- gie has come back to me!

Arrangement Copyright © 2008 Trudy Corporation

Notes and Nostalgia

The melody for the song *Oh Where, Oh Where Has My Little Dog Gone?* dates back to 1847 and was titled *Im Lauterbach hab'ich mein' Strumpf verlom* with lyrics about a lost sock. In 1864, a songwriter named Septimus Winner set English lyrics to the song and called it *Der Deichter's dog*, which later became *Oh Where, Oh Where Has My Little Dog Gone?*

In 1970, Winner was inducted into the Songwriters Hall of Fame.

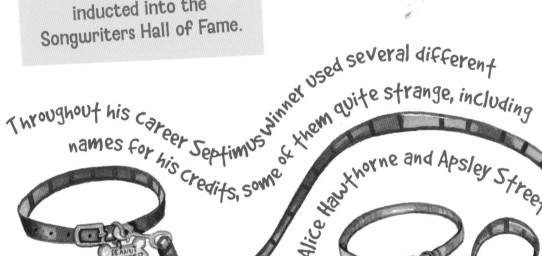

Throughout his career Septimus Winner used several different names for his credits, some of them quite strange, including Alice Hawthorne and Apsley Street.

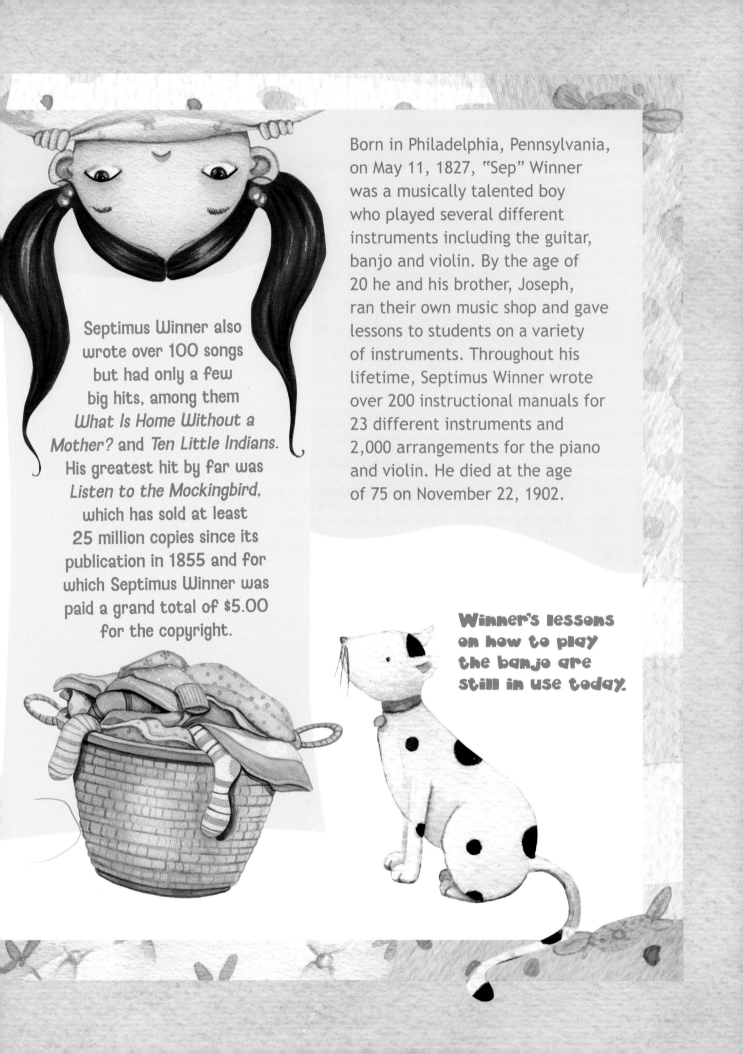

Born in Philadelphia, Pennsylvania, on May 11, 1827, "Sep" Winner was a musically talented boy who played several different instruments including the guitar, banjo and violin. By the age of 20 he and his brother, Joseph, ran their own music shop and gave lessons to students on a variety of instruments. Throughout his lifetime, Septimus Winner wrote over 200 instructional manuals for 23 different instruments and 2,000 arrangements for the piano and violin. He died at the age of 75 on November 22, 1902.

Septimus Winner also wrote over 100 songs but had only a few big hits, among them *What Is Home Without a Mother?* and *Ten Little Indians*. His greatest hit by far was *Listen to the Mockingbird*, which has sold at least 25 million copies since its publication in 1855 and for which Septimus Winner was paid a grand total of $5.00 for the copyright.

Winner's lessons on how to play the banjo are still in use today.

The first four lines of the song below are the original
Oh Where, Oh Where Has My Little Dog Gone? lyrics.
The last four lines of the song were written for
this book. You can try writing more lyrics, too.
What do you think happens when the dog comes home?

Oh where, oh where has my little dog gone?
Oh where, oh where can he be?
With his ears cut short and his tail cut long,
oh where, oh where can he be?

I love my doggie, oh so much,
and my doggie, I know he loves me.
He's my very best friend and I miss him so...LOOK!
My doggie has come back to me!